Antoine Laurain lives in Paris. His award-winning novels have been translated into fourteen languages and have sold more than 200,000 copies in English. *The President's Hat* was a Waterstones Book Club and Indies Introduce selection, and *The Red Notebook* was on the Indie Next list.

Le Sonneur is a contemporary Parisian artist. His work tells the story of Paris and the people who live there. His artwork is often placed in public spaces with an invitation to passers-by to interact with the work, for example by picking up a key or calling a telephone number.

Jane Aitken is a publisher and translator from the French.

Red Is My Heart

ANTOINE LAURAIN

Also by Antoine Laurain:

The Readers' Room
Vintage 1954
Smoking Kills
The Portrait
French Rhapsody
The Red Notebook
The President's Hat

Red Is My Heart

ANTOINE LAURAIN

Translated by Jane Aitken

Gallic Books

London

A Gallic Book

First published in France as *Et mon Cœur se serra*
by Flammarion, 2021
Copyright © Flammarion, Paris, 2021

English translation copyright © Gallic Books, 2022
First published in Great Britain in 2022 by
Gallic Books, 12 Eccleston Street
London, SW1W 9RT

A CIP record for this book is available from the British Library

ISBN 9781913547189

Printed in the UK by CPI (CR0 4YY)

2 4 6 8 10 9 7 5 3 1

T

oday I posted
you a letter, a very beautiful letter,
three carefully drafted pages written with a
medium-nib Cross fountain pen in black ink.
When I went to write your address on the envelope,
my hand trembled and I invented a new one.
An address that does not exist, a random
number in an imaginary street which I placed
in an arrondissement on the other side of the city.
8 Rue Pierre-François-Flarmentier, Paris 15.
I posted the letter in the yellow postbox.

You will never read it.

I wonder what will become of my envelope –
will someone at the post office open it and read
the three pages? Is there a procedure for letters
with neither recipient nor sender? I would
at least like a postal worker to take a few
minutes to frown in puzzlement, open the online
directory for that arrondissement and realise that Rue
Pierre-François-Flarmentier does not exist. How long
until the letter is destroyed? A few days, a month?
Will it end up in a wastepaper basket or in a shredder
that will turn it into long paper shavings? I must
try to find out.

I imagine what your flat in Rue Flarmentier is like:
huge, with parquet floors, full of light.
You sleep in a blue velvet bed. There isn't much
furniture – you're waiting for me to bring mine.

You're waiting for me. You're sleeping.
You'll wait for me all your life
in that apartment. You left.
You will be in Rue Pierre-François-Flarmentier for eternity.

I've met someone . . .
I'm leaving you, I don't
love you any more,
it's over, I still love you,
but it's over. You'll get
over it, time's a great
healer, you'll see.
We're done. I'm going.
I wish it hadn't come to
this, but life has come
between us . . . I don't even know what
you said any more.
In fact, I have no
recollection of anything
you said. All I remember
is that I understood it
was the end. That you
were leaving me. That
I would never see you
again, that we would
never be seen
together again.

You were shutting me out
    and my words could not reach you.
I pleaded my case but
    it was already closed: you had already left
    a long time ago and I had not realised, or
hadn't wanted to realise. That last conversation
was nothing more than a formality for you. Something you
just had to get through.
After which, you would go elsewhere, free. Find someone else,
maybe.
Definitely.
And what about me? Where would I go?
You plunge a knife in my heart yet you say
you do not wish to hurt me.
You say you're not responsible for the dagger. That
it's in the hands of destiny. You tell me that no one is to
blame.
I don't agree.

'Objection, *mon honneur.*'
'Objection, *mon amour.*'

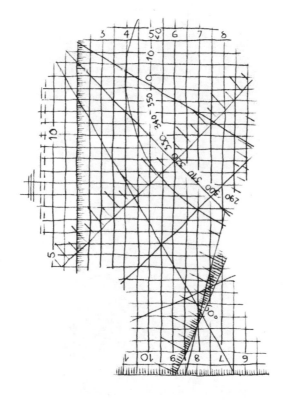

I'm going to change
my watch. A decision I
took suddenly at 4.14 in
the morning. I was pacing
the room as the coffee machine
roared – that system could really
do with improvement; the noise is
unbearable. Incidentally, I recently pur-
chased a silent vacuum cleaner that really
does clean and really is silent.

It's completely fascinating.

Leaving the relative noise level of household appliances aside, let's return to my watch. I'm going to change it. I feel that by changing my watch, I will change my concept of time. By buying a new watch, I will buy a new kind of time. A new kind of life. Mechanical watches are living objects; the workings beat against your wrist. The heart of my watch beat too hard for you and I want a new heart, from a different brand with a new face. I will put my current watch in a drawer and strap the new watch to my wrist. I will look at the brand-new hands, and at the second hand passing the new numbers. Everything about it will be new. If I hold the face to my ear, I will hear the ticking and it will symbolise renewal. From now on, there will be a new Greenwich Mean Time just for me.

You will be far away, **in another time zone**. A zone that is only relevant to my old watch – at the back of a dark drawer.

Can you change the path of love by changing your watch?

I did not change my watch.

A crime was committed in my street.

Madame Séraphine, the widow
of the wine merchant François Lemarchand, was
found strangled in her apartment.
Her jewellery had been stolen. It was the building
just next door to mine.
I am very shocked by this event.
It happened on 2 February 1889.
Le Journal Illustré put it on their cover with a drawing
that looked like an old engraving. You could see
the beautiful Séraphine Lemarchand lying on the floor
in disarray, and a man holding a candelabra – presumably
the concierge or a neighbour
– opening a door and finding the body.
There was a look of stupefaction on his face.

Since you've been gone, I haven't
known what to do with my nights so
I searched for my street on eBay. Several
old black-and-white postcards appeared, along
with that copy of *Le Journal Illustré*. I ordered it
immediately and it has just arrived this morning.

I went to the florist's, chose a bouquet
and asked for it to be delivered to the address
in my street for the attention of Séraphine
Lemarchand. I requested it be left in the hall of
the apartment building with this card: 'For Séraphine
Lemarchand, with best wishes from a neighbour.' The
young woman serving me made no comment on this singular
request. But she did ask me for the entry code to the building. I
told her I didn't have it. She checked on her system. They had
delivered flowers to that address a short while ago. So they had
the code. I paid and left.

I can no longer
bring you flowers.
I send flowers to a
woman who died in 1889.
I am the only person
who still thinks of her.

Was her killer ever found?

Perhaps I would have been happy
with Séraphine?

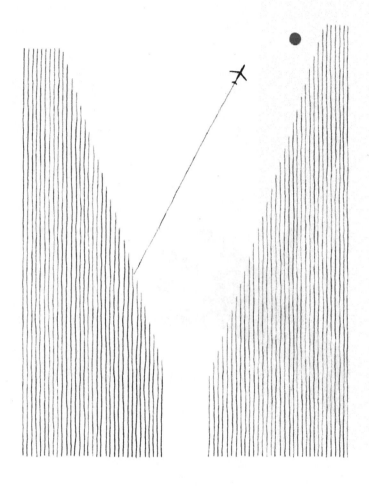

I'm a little tired of starting
with that phrase.

I'm thinking of devising a sort of
variant of the usual calendar which is based
around the birth of Christ. Mine will start
with your departure. So I am in the early part
of year 1 after you. YR1 AY . . .

I have always thought there was a certain
     charm in living in the early days
          of an era. Now I'm not
                    so sure . . .

The early days of life without you seem like dark times, full of forests, wolves, witches and paths that lead nowhere in the pouring rain.

Since you've been gone, as I was saying, I find it hard to sleep. I wake every morning at precisely ten past four. I have researched this phenomenon. It's called 'adjustment insomnia', and it normally lasts at least three months. It falls into the category of 'acute, short-term insomnia, associated with a stressful event – psychological, environmental, physical or psychosocial'.

It is said to stop when the causal factor is removed or when the person adapts.

You are the causal factor. I do not see how your removal from my heart and mind is possible. Nor do I envisage adapting. So I do seriously envisage waking at 4.10 a.m. for the rest of my life.

Continuing my research, I came across
a very interesting article. Which unfor-
tunately I will not be able to share with
you. It puts forward the theory – tested
out on willing participants – that suffering
follows a very precise timetable. Waking at
three in the morning is said to happen after a
bereavement, waking at four after a break-up,
at five o'clock when you have money worries,
and so on. There is a night-time schedule of
unhappiness.

And that is the schedule I am now on.

How do you get to sleep when I'm not there?

What about you, how are you sleeping?

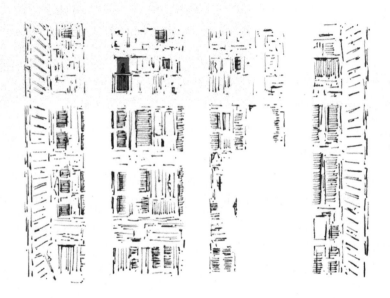

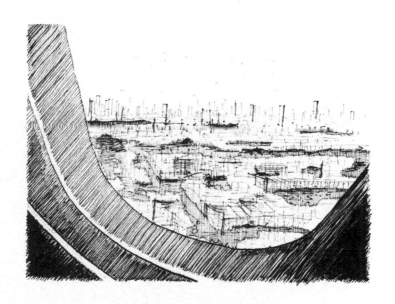

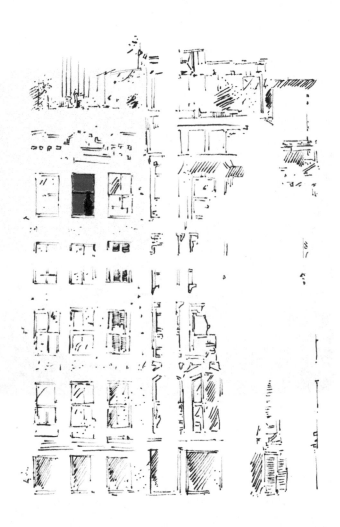

Today I walked
the streets.
Walked *my* streets, I should
say, since I never leave
the neighbourhood. My range
has shrunk. I went along
the street with the electricity
substation – the gates are painted
grey. There's a sign with
a very clear message:

Smoking is strictly prohibited inside or outside this building.

A police car stopped on the other
side of the street, just opposite.

The police got out. There were four of them, two using walkie-talkies. I took out my cigarettes, stood in front of the sign and lit one, taking large puffs while looking them in the eye.

SMOKING IS STRICTLY PROHIBITED . . .

None of them paid me the slightest attention. They didn't even glance at me. I was expecting one of them to cross the road and challenge me: 'Can't you read? Do you know where you are?'

'Show me your papers,' is a phrase that would have filled me with happiness just then.

'Follow me,' would have been even more exciting.

For them to have made me get into their car, revolving light flashing and siren blaring, to take me to the station and slap a fine on me, would have been the most marvellous distraction of my day. At least I wouldn't be thinking about you.

Nothing happened. They went back the way they had come.

I stubbed my cigarette out on the
pavement.

I no longer exist.

Even the police don't want anything to do with me.

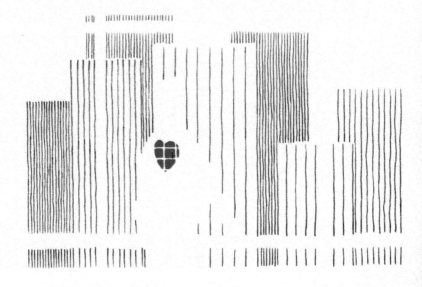

50

The last time we spoke,

I was wearing a grey jacket. That grey jacket is not in
itself important

but I have just allocated it a key role in our relationship

and I have been thinking about it since
4.15 this morning.

Every time we argued, then separated, I was wearing that
jacket.

I'm sure of it. I have other jackets: black, dark grey, denim,
velvet. But it was always that one
I was wearing whenever we split up. At our last,
        final break-up, I was wearing it again.

I have just put it on a chair and I'm looking at it as I drink my coffee. It is impossible for that jacket and me to continue living together. And right now I want to write you a message to tell you that all this is nothing to do with us, it's all the jacket's fault. Not mine, not yours. I bought it years ago, long before I met you, but its malign power only became apparent after you came into my life. To think that I looked after that evil jacket by taking it to the dry-cleaner's and hanging it carefully in the wardrobe when all the time it was waiting for the opportunity to turn against me. I have no memory of the shop assistant who got me to try it on – all smiles, I expect, but they say the devil has a winning smile.

I'm going
to go out, wearing
another jacket but taking that
one with me. I'm going to hook it
over the parking meter in my street, using
the machine like a clothes hanger, and then I'm
going to get in the car.

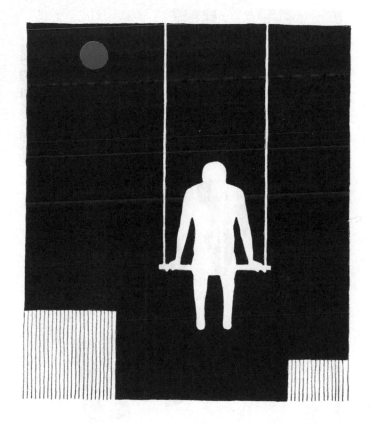

I came back this
evening. There was
nothing hanging on
the parking meter.

The jacket had
disappeared.

This morning, as I opened the curtains, I saw a chest of drawers go past my window. A removal ladder had been set up, very early, and I had heard nothing. One of those electric ladders with a platform that goes up and down. My upstairs neighbour, Monsieur Marsellier, was moving out. He had pinned me under a ladder. I always avoid ladders when I'm in the street. But he had condemned me to spend several hours under a huge electric ladder as it carried his furniture down for all to see.

I don't know where or when the superstition about ladders comes from. I once read – but I'm not sure I believe it – that fear of ladders comes from ancient Egypt because a ladder against a wall forms a triangle. Ra (the god of the sun, if I remember correctly) was represented by a triangle. So to pass through a triangle was a blasphemy of the worst kind. It meant passing through the representation of the body of the supreme god of that polytheistic religion. Personally, I think the superstition about ladders has a much more prosaic explanation. Often, painters are perched at the top of ladders, so if you walk under them you run the risk of being splashed with paint.

Either way, the ladder propped in front of my window so enraged me that I shouted, 'You bastard, Marsellier!' in my sitting room. Very loudly. The next minute I was seized with panic. I thought my neighbour was going to come and knock on my door. I locked it. And I waited, terrified. In vain. No one came.

When I came home this evening, the electric ladder had disappeared. Marsellier would never be my neighbour again. There was no sign in the street of his recent removal. There would be no trace of Marsellier in the building, other than his name on the register of co-owners, which would soon be forgotten. There had been a red cloth on the ladder; I saw it this morning, going up and down outside my window, over and over again. The wind must have blown it away. Now it's stuck in the shutter of the building opposite. It's strange to see it there.

How long will it be there? It's like a cry for help. No one will come and collect it. It will fall down, eventually, and end up in a bin, then on a rubbish dump, torn to pieces by the seagulls that hover above these places.

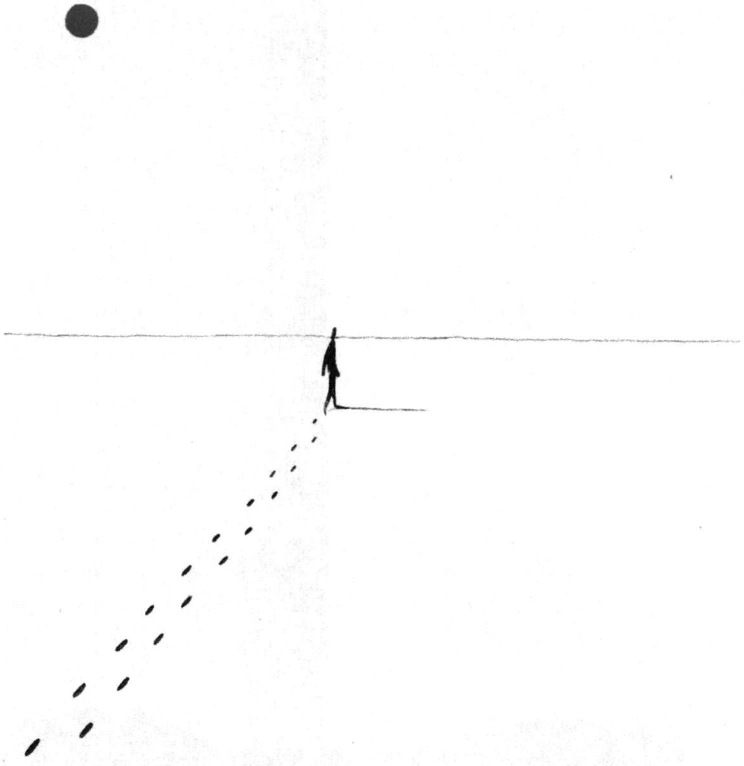

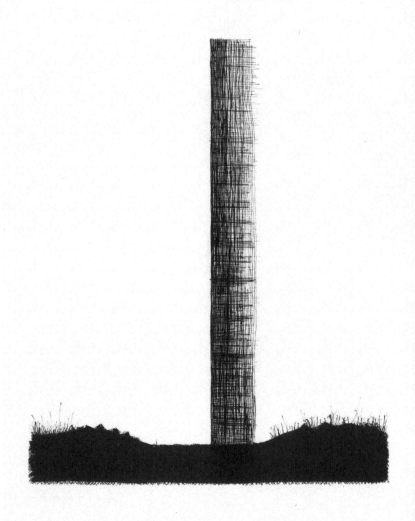

I'm sitting on the terrace of my café.

I say my café, but it's not mine, it's everyone's.
It's just the one I go to. I have chosen it and
I don't really know why. I've decided to go
there at weekends from now on, to be on the
terrace at precisely ten o'clock, like going to
work. I stay for an hour, doing absolutely
nothing other than watching the world go by
around me. I now feel separate, or excluded
from what's going on. I have become a tourist,
a mere visitor to this earth where I have not
found, nor ever hope to find my place.

I look up at the sound of fire-engine sirens. There is a whole procession of vehicles. The large fire engine with the ladder on top is followed by two smaller ones, and two police cars. What tragedy is unfolding in the city as I drink my coffee? Has an apartment been blown apart by a gas explosion? Or a building caught fire? Has some extremist – to use the accepted term – locked himself in somewhere with a hand gun and a knife to defy the world? Is some desperate soul standing on their roof threatening to jump? Those firemen should have parked their engines outside my café and come to see me. They would have asked my name. And added, 'Don't try to fight it, you've been in very bad shape recently and we're here to help.' I would not have put up a fight, they would have unfolded the stretcher on wheels, laid me on it, then put an oxygen mask on my face. There would have been an army of people to look after me in the red fire engine with the ladder as it whizzed through the city.

The police would have followed to make sure everything was all right. On arrival at the hospital, the police would have questioned me:

'Who has hurt you so badly?' I would have given your name.

'We'll take care of her,' they would have said.

'I have faith in you, *messieurs*, and in the law of my country,' I would have replied before slipping into unconsciousness.

I'm going to order another coffee.

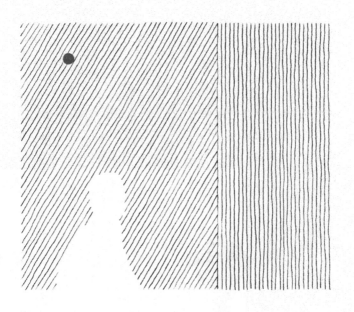

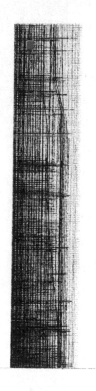

I went past
the shop where I
bought your fur-lined
boots. Beige suede
with a sort of white
sheepskin inside
that you could either wear
turned right down or just
at the top to make a cuff.
The boots were for our
Swedish trip four months
ago. Guess what –
the shop has closed.
It's been replaced
by an organic
greengrocer.

You were away
for work,
and I absolutely
had to find you
that pair of boots
before you returned
the evening before
our departure
for Sweden.

I went to several shoe shops in the area, told them your size and looked at different styles to check their quality and durability. I told them they were 'for my wife'. Just for fun. We weren't married but you were my wife nevertheless. Perhaps we should have got married. Out of the blue, without thinking about it. Perhaps you wouldn't have left. That thought came to me at 4.15 in the morning a few nights ago.

I looked through the window into the new shop. I did not have the strength to go in. Where I had spotted your fur lined boots, there was now a display of courgettes. People were going in and out as if this had always been a greengrocer. I have never bought fur-lined boots. That shoe shop never existed.

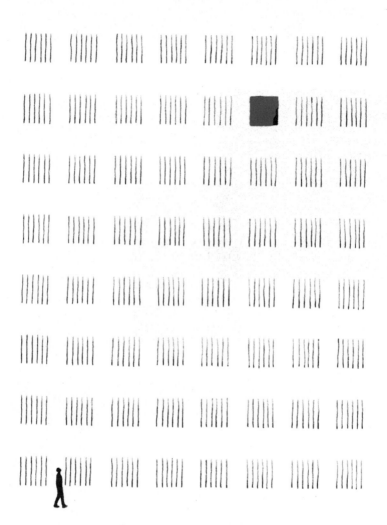

81

Yesterday, I tapped in the entry code
for your building.
B7634.

And I went in.
I was certain you weren't there.
It was mid-afternoon on a Thursday. No,
you could not be there, although a slight
element of doubt lingered. But even more than
that sense of doubt, which did, of course, worry
me, it was another feeling that predominated,
the feeling of now being like a thief or criminal
in a place so familiar to me.

Everything made me uncomfortable: the stairs, the radiator, the letterboxes, the corridor leading to the courtyard where we put out the bins. The lift that could be called at any time. Everything had suddenly become hostile. The hall that I had crossed with you hundreds of times and which had always been so welcoming because it symbolised the start of an evening spent together, or a night, or an afternoon. Nothing in the decor had changed, but it was now a source of terror and the space also seemed to be afraid of me. Its deafening silence was a rejection. And I almost had the impression that the front door would open and I would see us coming in – both of us – as in happier times, carrying shopping, discussing this and that. You would be laughing, and so would I. And I would have watched us, without either of us seeing me.

It was unbelievable that the smiling man on your arm, who carried the shopping through the hall, could have become this pale ghost, standing immobile in this place which now frightened him.

Your
name
is
still on
the intercom.
On the
letterbox.
You still
live here.

I left abruptly
and walked for a long time.

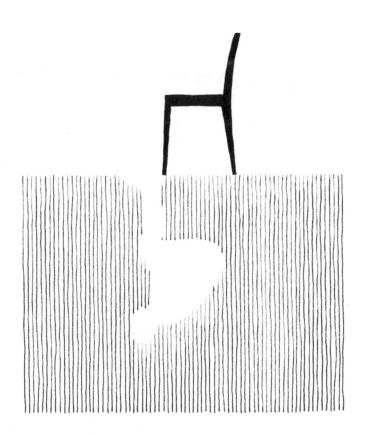

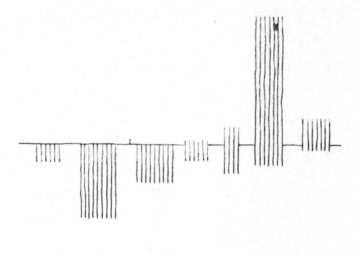

This evening, I'm roaming, going from bar to bar.
I begin with certain bars in my neighbourhood
that I know and where I am known. I'm going to
continue, going in concentric circles through the
city. Circles which will have the same centre without
necessarily the same diameter – the centre, of course,
is my home. Dante also conceived a system of circles
in his *Inferno* – which, by the way, I have never read.
My circles will be less theological than the Florentine's.
They will be called Gin Fizz, Americano, Bloody Mary,
Mojito . . . and my hell will consist of ending up dead
drunk in front of barmen who refuse to serve me. I will
then take a taxi back to the centre of the circle: home.

There's one thing I like about Dante, not that I know much about him. He met his Beatrice one afternoon and never saw her again. He raved about her for the rest of his life. His whole life based on one afternoon. He was consumed by love for someone he had never kissed, never held in his arms.

In fact, for a woman he knew nothing about.

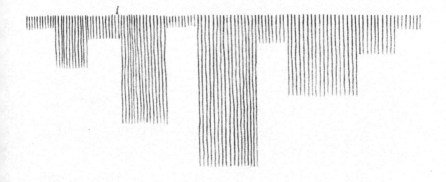

I woke up
in my bed this morning.

After the fifth
circle,
I have no
memory
of what
happened.

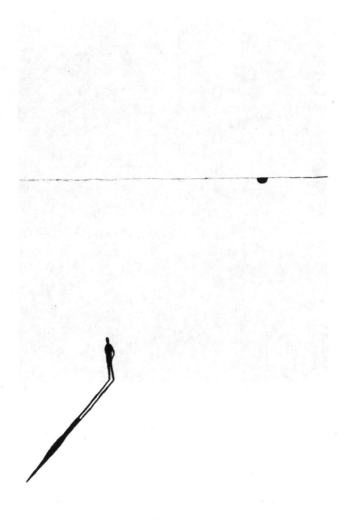

What did
I ever see in
her?

If I meet you by chance
in the street in ten or fifteen
years and we exchange a few words,
even have coffee, will I ask that question
about you? I have bumped into an ex-lover
before. And wondered why I had been so taken
with her when we were together. And the opposite
must also be true. Surely the woman must have asked
herself what she ever saw in me.

Emptiness,
loss, pain and injustice
would all disappear, pushed aside by
that unseemly question. I find the idea of
that utterly horrifying. I won't allow it.

It won't happen. I can't admit that time
smooths over everything, that rain washes
away feeling, that wind changes the shape
of rocks. In ten years, in a thousand
years, I will not have changed my
opinion. I will know exactly
what I saw in you.

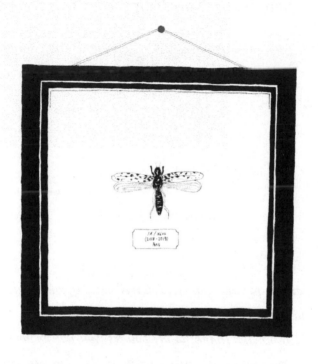

Yesterday I took the metro. On the seat there was a photocopy of a business card.

Professor Habibou

Famous medium, discreet clairvoyant. If you want to find love or your partner has met someone else, I can help! Thanks to my powers, you will be loved again and find perfect harmony. All your problems will be solved. Protection from evil spirits, exam success, remedies for impotence. Discretion assured. By appointment. Remote bookings also offered. Include SAE.

The advert ended with two mobile numbers and the name of a metro station in a working-class district of Paris.

Professor Habibou must live in one of those hidden spots in the city; one of those streets you never go to that make you wonder if they really exist. Perhaps I should go and see him and talk to him about you. Perhaps the age-old witchcraft used by mystics could come to my aid? I thought about that as I travelled. I tried to imagine my first meeting with the professor. I tried to envisage his clients, probably all sorts of people, all in search of rapid solutions to their problems. The professor must possess the gifts of his ancestors going back at least fifteen generations. It was all completely fascinating: perhaps I had found the solution to all my troubles on this small rectangle of paper.

I took

the paper.

I threw it

in a bin

as I left

the station.

I've continued researching men who were madly in love with women they barely knew.

Of course, I did know you; we had a long relationship, but the phenomenon interests me. Who knows why. I came across Alain-Fournier, the author of *Le Grand Meaulnes*, the cult novel everyone is made to read at school. The famous author died young in the Great War. At what age did I read him? Thirteen or fourteen? My memory is of a very beautiful, long, slow novel which I found extremely boring at the time. The facts: on 1 June 1905, Alain-Fournier has just visited the Salon National des Beaux-Arts.

He's going down the stairs of the Petit Palais when he notices a blonde girl, tall, elegant and slender, dressed in a brown coat. She glances at him in passing.

Alain-Fournier is eighteen, and a student at the Lycée Lakanal when he crosses paths with the beautiful stranger. Shortly after the writer's death, his friend and schoolfellow Jacques Rivière said, 'That brief encounter was the defining moment of his life and a source of immense passion, sadness and rapture.'

Without knowing who she is, Alain-Fournier follows Yvonne Toussaint de Quièvrecourt as she walks towards the Seine. She boards a Bateau-Mouche and alights at Quai de la Tournelle to return to her parents' apartment at 12 Boulevard Saint Germain, still pursued at a distance by the lovestruck young man. In the days that follow, he keeps returning to that address to try to see her again. Finally, on the morning of 10 June, he spots her at the window of the apartment. The girl, surprised to see him, smiles warmly.

The next morning, he waits for her to come out. There she is, prayer book in hand. He steels himself and whispers, 'You're beautiful,' to her just before she gets onto the tram.

He follows her.

At the end of Mass, he approaches her. This time she agrees to speak to him. They take a tram going to Pont des Invalides. They are finally talking. Sitting near her, Alain-Fournier feverishly writes in a notebook. At Pont de la Concorde, they get off and part, having exchanged names. The girl has told him she is engaged to be married. As she leaves, she asks him not to follow her any more, then turns round. They exchange a long look.

That's the end of the encounter. Alain-Fournier will never get over it.

Eight years later he publishes *Le Grand Meaulnes* – a masterpiece that passed me by. We will never know if Yvonne really read it. He saw her a few times years later. She was married with two children. It was completely hopeless. She offered a friendship he had no interest in. He had failed at love and very probably at life. He suffered. But his suffering was cut short by the Great War. He was killed on 22 September 1914, along with his entire unit. His body was identified in a communal grave in 1991.

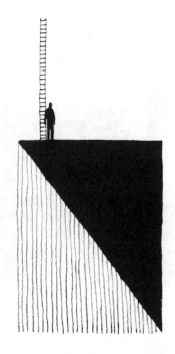

I followed
  the route
    Alain-Fournier had
      taken through Paris
        in pursuit of Yvonne.
      But saw only
        tourists
          and
            walkers.

I read in a scientific article that the sun is expanding. It's getting bigger and that's very worrying. Eventually it will become so enormous that it will collapse in on itself. The article said, 'In roughly five billion years, our sun will be in its red giant phase and will swallow all the planets in the solar system.'

So one day the earth will be swallowed by the sun. That seems to be a given. It's getting closer to the sun and one day will be inside it. Global warming, which will lead to drought and then intolerable heat, will eradicate all traces of life.

The silent earth will advance
inexorably towards the star
of light and what is left
of us will catch fire: books,
cupboards, tables,
desks, shelves.
Then it will be buildings,
towers, roads
and motorways. Earth
will get close to the sun,
be swallowed up and
fizzle out.

I found that thought rather
comforting. Why should we go
to all this trouble if one day the earth
will be swallowed by the sun and there
will be nothing left?

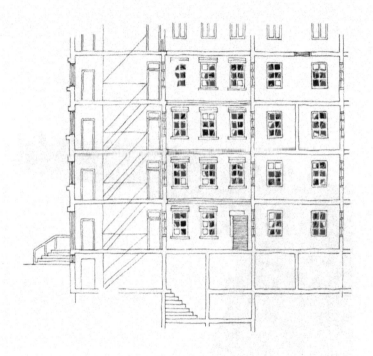

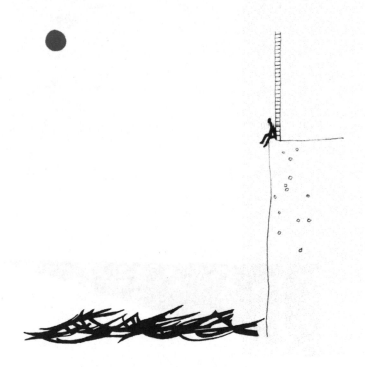

I move about inside your apartment. I am like a shaman enjoying an out-of-body experience. All I have to do is sit in my armchair and close my eyes. I wonder if you look up for a moment, if perhaps you have the impression, for a fraction of a second, that a shadow has passed through the room. I pass your wardrobe mirror; it's surreal how sharp everything is; I can even smell the coffee you used to make in the morning as I slept on. I feel the wooden bannister of the stairs leading down from the mezzanine under my left hand and the tiles under my bare feet. I am really at your place. I can go from the sitting room to the bathroom to the kitchen. I can open the French window and look at the trees.

If I can
be there

so vividly

through the power of thought,

I must really be there.

I have thrown everything away. I have thrown everything of yours away. Everything of us. That bird keyring we'll never put our keys on. I threw away the records you gave me, the LPs. I threw away the books, the pencils. I threw away the clothes you left behind. And those you advised me to buy. I want there to be nothing left. I took down the photo of you I had pinned on the wall and I thought, 'If anyone had ever told me I would remove this picture and tear it into pieces . . .' But that day has arrived. I have been even more radical with the computer. I deleted all the folders containing our photos.

'Empty trash?'
enquired my computer.
Yes.
No.

I pressed yes. A blue bar like a horizontal thermometer appeared and filled up slowly then disappeared from my screen. There is nothing left of our trips or the hundreds of photos I took of you without you knowing. Hundreds of photos that you never saw. No one will ever see them now. Not even me.
They no longer exist.
I threw away the hard drive.
It had cost 54.98 euros.

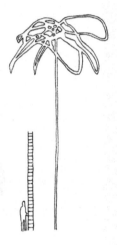

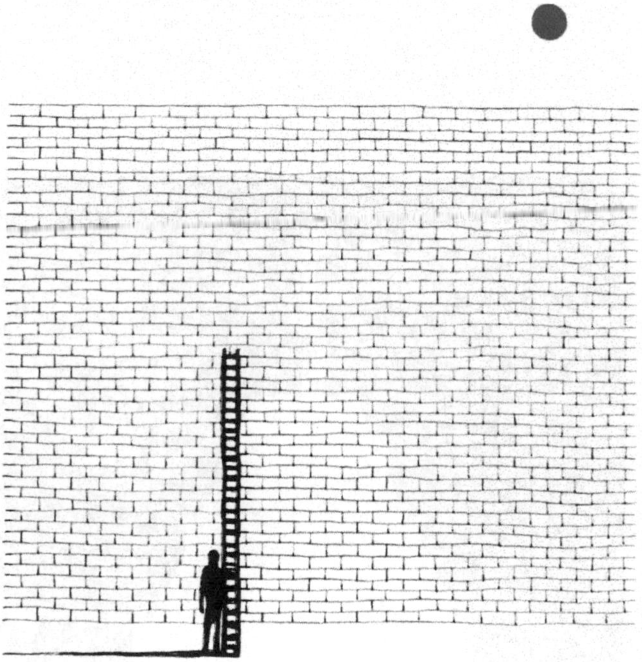

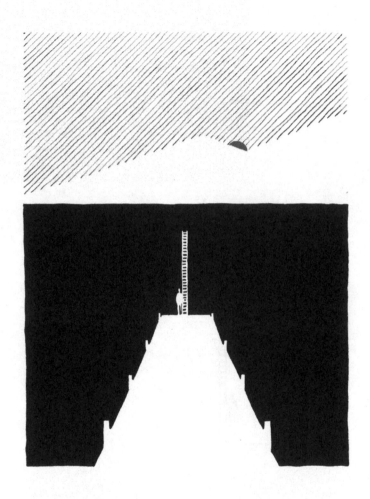

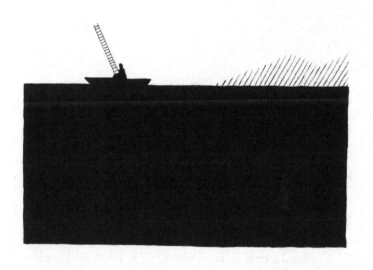

We were supposed to be going to
New York tomorrow. I bought the
tickets months in advance. I'm going to
check us in; I want them to call our names
at the airport.
I want there to be one last time
when our names are announced together over a
loudspeaker. Tomorrow, at work, I will look at my
watch as the departure gate is closing.

Under the large dome of Roissy Charles-de-Gaulle, our names will be called, along with, 'are requested to come immediately to gate 16.'

'Are requested . . .'

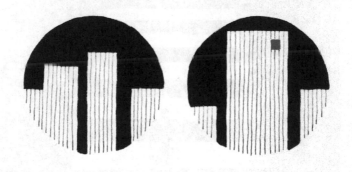

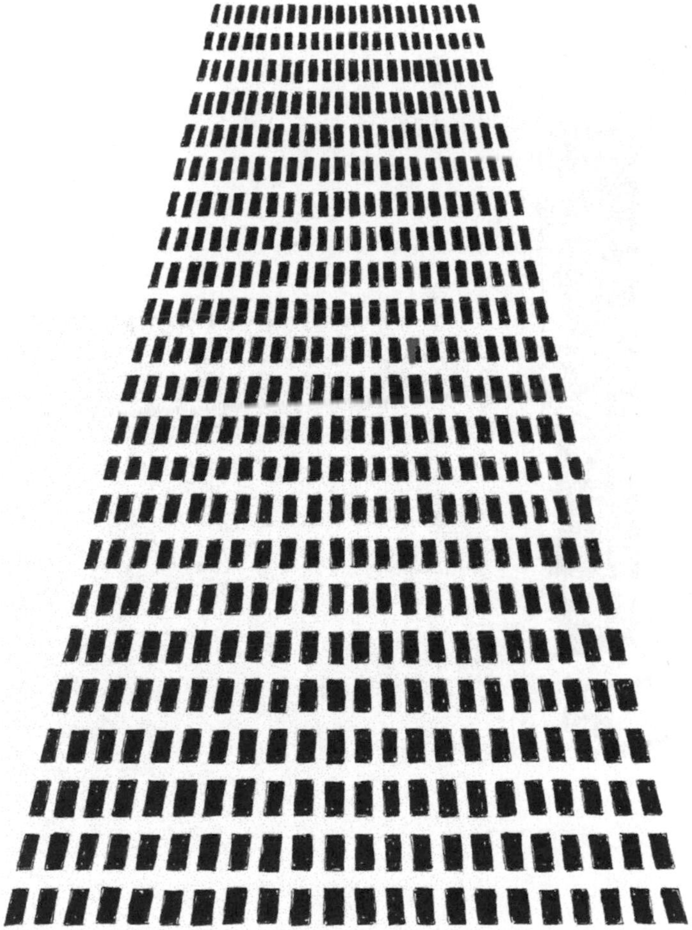

There's a plaque saying
'Mon amour' in my street.
A golden brass plaque of
the kind you see outside a
lawyer's office or a doctor's
surgery. The plaque has
the number of the floor
followed by a phone
number. The plaque is
shiny and brand new. I
stood in front of it for
a long time looking at
my reflection in the gold
metal.

It was stated that the
love in question
was available by
appointment.

Was it really a company called
Mon Amour or a piece of performance
        art by a contemporary artist?

Perhaps I was being filmed? I would find myself
    in an art installation video which would be
        shown all over the world from Dubai
            to Tokyo unbeknownst to me.

                        I left hurriedly.

The next day the plaque had disappeared. It was an artist.
I looked on the internet and I found him. It was Le Sonneur.
His face is not well-known. He puts up plaques,
slips envelopes underneath doors or sticks
fake doorbells underneath intercoms.

His art does not last and serves no purpose.

I could be friends with someone like that.

I found another interesting article in the scientific review that had forecast that in the near future – five billion years hence – the earth would be swallowed by the sun, and it was about LHRH.

Or gonadotrophin-releasing hormone. Which is secreted in the hypothalamus, in the brain. This hormone means that when we go in search of someone to love, our body prepares itself to love. Or perhaps it's the opposite; when we are in love, our hypothalamus secretes LHRH, which predisposes us to focus on the object of our love. Scientists disagree on which it is but the effects are the same. Under the influence of LHRH, we stop feeling yearning, and we are less interested in the outside world. We are fixated only on the one we love. This blissfully happy, floating state of love, according to numerous scientific studies, lasts a limited time.

LHRH is only effective for ninety days.

After that, you become aware of the faults of the loved one, daily life takes over and the yearning returns.

In short, real love
only lasts three months.

I threw the magazine away.
I don't agree with it.
LHRH lasts much
longer and the earth
is not round, it is flat.
The oceans fall like
waterfalls into the cosmos.
That's why so many
ships disappear.

Today

I noted down

this sentence:

Of

all we

have

lived,

nothing remains

but the

memory of

a dream.

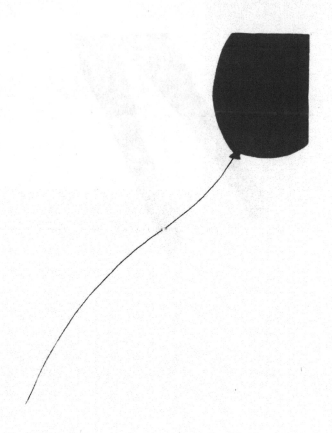

A
week after
    I noted down that sentence,
       I write another:

               Today a woman smiled at me
                      in the street.

This afternoon in the dentist's waiting room,
I flicked through a women's magazine
and came to a questionnaire which
I filled out.

'If you were reincarnated, what would you like to
come back as?'

I don't wish to be reincarnated.

'What is your idea of happiness?'

No idea.

'Where would you like to go for your next holiday?'

Nowhere.

'Are you concerned for the future of the planet?'

No, it will end up inside the sun.

'What do you think of when you look at a flower?'
Nothing. I don't look at flowers.
'Would you prefer to live in the city or in the country?'
Neither.
'If you could change something about
your appearance, what would it be?'
Everything.
'The last time you laughed was . . .'
So long ago, I don't remember.
'Do you sing in the shower?'
I have a bath.

None of my responses corresponded to any of the answers suggested by the magazine, so I wrote them in the margin with the Cross ballpoint pen you gave me. I was called for my appointment and wasn't able to finish the questionnaire. Once you had answered all the questions, you were told which of the three personality types you fitted.I think I belong to a fourth category, not among those suggested. It's for the best.

I also left the Cross pen inside the magazine.

I'm on a café terrace,
waiting for the woman who smiled at
me. We've bumped into each other
at the newspaper kiosk three times.

It's Saturday, 17.57 GMT.

She'll be here soon. I don't know
whether I will stay, or go before she
arrives. It's eight months since you
left. I would like it to be you who turns
up and yet, at the same time, I have to
admit, I don't really want that any more.
I'm going to go with the flow. I feel as
if I am looking at the world through
a keyhole and what I see scares me.

Yet I must open the door. The woman from the kiosk appears at the end of the road. Will she be a source of happiness or suffering? Are we going to live together for the next few years or will everything stop after our coffee? Anything is possible. I think of LHRH, of the bin bag containing all your possessions, of the holiday photos erased from my hard drive, of the letter I sent to you at Rue Pierre-François-Flarmentier, of Séraphine Lemarchand . . . My mind is buzzing.

I am ready for anything.

I'm not ready for anything.

And the woman approaches.

She smiles at me.

I find her beautiful.

'Bonsoir . . .'

'Bonsoir . . .'